KINJI
GOES FISHING

KINJI
GOES FISHING

by Harriet Johnson
Illustrated by Leo Summers

Edith G. Stull, General Editor

THE L. W. SINGER COMPANY
A Division of Random House, Inc.
Syracuse • Atlanta • Chicago • Dallas • Menlo Park

One bright blue morning Kinji decided
to go fishing.

He took a tall bamboo pole
with a long string and a sharp hook
on the end.

He took a tall tin can
with three smelly shrimp in it for bait.

And he started out.

Just as he came to the door,
his mother called:

"Kinji, please take out the trash
before you go."

So Kinji put down the tall bamboo pole
with a long string and a sharp hook
on the end.
   He put down the tall tin can
with three smelly shrimp in it for bait.
   He took out the trash.

"Thank you, Kinji," said his mother.

She gave him two sandwiches
in a brown bag.

"Have a good time," she said.

Just as Kinji was going out the door,
his sister called:

"Kinji, will you get me a box
to stand on?

I want to pick flowers for a lei
from the tree."

So Kinji put down the tall bamboo pole
with a long string and a sharp hook
on the end.

He put down the tall tin can
with three smelly shrimp in it for bait.

And he put down the brown bag
with the two sandwiches.

He found a box for his sister
to stand on.

"Thank you, little monkey,"
said his sister.

She gave him a ukulele to play
while he waited for the fish to bite.

"Have a good time," she said.

Kinji went as far as the white gate
when his father called:
"Oh, Kinji, will you turn on the hose
so I can water the flowers?"

So Kinji put down the tall bamboo pole
with the long string and the sharp hook
on the end.

He put down the tall tin can
with three smelly shrimp in it for bait.

He put down the brown bag
with the two sandwiches.

He put down the ukulele to play
while he waited for the fish to bite.

He turned on the hose for his father.

"Thank you, Kinji," said his father.

He gave Kinji a bottle of cool water
to drink when he was thirsty.

"Have a good time," he said.

Kinji went through the gate
and started down the road.
Before he had gone very far,
he met his Aunty Momi.

"I am so happy to see you, Kinji,"
she said.
"Will you hold this pot of poi for me
so I can take the stone out of my shoe?"

So Kinji put down the tall bamboo pole
with the long string and the sharp hook
on the end.

He put down the tall tin can
with three smelly shrimp in it for bait.

He put down the brown bag
with the two sandwiches.

He put down the ukulele to play
while he waited for the fish to bite.

He put down the bottle of cool water
to drink when he was thirsty.

He held the pot of poi for his aunty.

"Thank you, Kinji," said his aunty.

She put a big hat on his head
to keep the sun out of his eyes.

"Have a good time," she said.

Kinji walked up the road
to the top of the hill.
Bump-bang! Bump-bang! Bump-bang!
Up the hill came Kinji's brother, Tom,
in his old Juk-a-luca truck.

"Kinji! Kinji!" called Tom,
stopping the truck.

"Please look under the truck and
see what is going bump-bang-bump."

So Kinji put down the tall bamboo pole
with the long string and the sharp hook
on the end.

He put down the tall tin can
with three smelly shrimp in it for bait.

He put down the brown bag
with the two sandwiches.

He put down the ukulele to play
while he waited for the fish to bite.

He put down the bottle of cool water
to drink when he was thirsty.

And he took off the big hat that he had
on his head to keep the sun out of his eyes.

He looked under the old Juk-a-luca truck.

He couldn't see anything and said so.

"Thank you, little alligator,"
said his brother.

He gave Kinji a red and white candy
to eat as he went down to the sea.

"Have a good time," he said.

Kinji put the candy in his mouth and
it lasted all the way to the sea.

The sea was blue, the sky was bright,
and the sun was very hot
when Kinji sat down to fish.

Kinji tipped the big hat
that his Aunty Momi put on his head
to keep the sun out of his eyes.

He drank some of the cool water
that his father gave him to drink
when he was thirsty.

He ate the two sandwiches
that were in the brown bag.
Then Kinji played the ukulele
while he waited for the fish to bite.

And with the three smelly shrimp
on the sharp hook on the end
of the long string on the tall bamboo pole
Kinji caught three fat fish.